There's Something in There

by Sherry Shahan

text illustrations by Estella Lee Hickman

To Daddy,
for teaching me to ride a wave
farther than the boys

Published by Willowisp Press, Inc.
401 E. Wilson Bridge Road, Worthington , Ohio 43085

Printed in the United States of America
10 9 8 7 6 5 4 3 2 1

ISBN 0-87406-381-7

One

RACHEL Henson checked the clock on the stove. It was 3:15. The mail would be delivered any minute. She tucked her hair inside her knitted cap and slipped her fingers into her mittens. *I feel lucky today*, she thought. *Today's mail will bring a letter from Daddy.*

Rachel raced out the door and down the slippery walkway. "Is there anything for me today?" she called. "I'm waiting for something from California."

Mr. Martin stopped his three-wheeled cart on a sheet of thin ice. He reached into the dark blue satchel that was stamped US MAIL in red lettering. "Here's one from TX!" he shouted, saying the letters separately—tee

3

ex—as he checked the names and addresses. Mr. Martin shouted because he was wearing earmuffs and couldn't hear. *That's how everyone in the neighborhood knew everyone else's business*, Rachel decided as she watched him sort through the envelopes.

"That's easy," she said. Rachel and Mr. Martin were playing the post office guessing game that they'd made up. "It's Texas. Give me a harder one. I *am* in the fifth grade, you know."

"Okay, okay," Mr. Martin laughed. "How about PR?"

Rachel thought for a moment. The only state beginning with a *P* that she could think of was Pennsylvania and its abbreviation was PA. "It's Puerto Rico," she said finally.

"That's very good!"

Rachel smiled.

"I bet it's easier to deliver mail to houses than to apartments," she said, looking down both sides of the street. Apartments reminded

4

her of empty milk cartons stacked one on top of the other. Mr. Martin held out a small stack of envelopes and read the return addresses. "All we ever get in the mail are bills," Rachel said sadly.

"Do you know Mrs. Jaeckel, who lives across the street?" Mr. Martin asked.

Rachel knew Mrs. Jaeckel and her cat Freddie Fantastic. Rachel helped Mrs. Jaeckel every week by carrying Freddie's cat box down the back stairs and dumping it in the garbage bin. Mrs. Jaeckel gave Rachel 50 cents each week for her help, so Rachel added two dollars a month to her coffee-can fund.

"She gets mail-in offers at the grocery store, and she sends labels to food companies," Mr. Martin said. "Then she receives coupons in the mail. Sometimes it's a two-for-one offer for tomato paste. Other times it's a 50-cent coupon for a box of Cracker Jacks."

Rachel pictured Mrs. Jaeckel eating Cracker Jacks. *How can she eat the nuts with one of her bottom teeth missing?* wondered Rachel.

"It's not what's in the mail that matters to Mrs. Jaeckel. It's having something to open," Mr. Martin explained.

Rachel thought about the letter she'd been expecting from her father. And she thought about what it would say.

Dearest Rachel:

I'm sorry I haven't written sooner, but my new job has been keeping me very busy. I'm enclosing a check for this month's rent, and an extra $20 for that skirt you want to buy. I love you very much, and I think of you often.

Hugs and kisses,

Daddy

P.S. Tell your mother I'm sorry about the argument.

Rachel cupped her fingers over her mouth and blew hot air into her wool mittens. "I guess it takes the mail a long time to get here from California to Illinois," she said.

"Don't give up. Maybe it'll come tomorrow!"

Mr. Martin shouted as he continued on his delivery route. Rachel watched him disappear around the corner.

Rachel turned and walked up the walkway. She thought about the argument that her parents had last month after she had gone to bed. She wasn't sure what it was all about. But it ended with her dad slamming the front door and driving away in their old car. Rachel tried to pull the covers so tightly over her head that she couldn't hear their angry voices and the breaking dishes. But the covers couldn't keep out the sound of the door slamming. Rachel thought it was the loudest and saddest sound she had ever heard. She had cried herself to sleep. And when she woke up the next morning, her father was gone.

"He went to California to find a job that pays more money," her mother explained the morning after the fight. "He'll send for us later."

They'd always fought about money, Rachel thought. *That's one problem I won't have when I grow up. I'm going to make a lot of money.*

Then Rachel heard the door to the storage shed in the Henson's carport banging in the wind. The noise brought her thoughts back to the present. The screws had fallen out of the hinges, and the door was hanging sideways. She was cold, standing outside in the chilly wind. "The coldest March in Illinois history," the man on the radio had said earlier. "The windchill factor is 13 degrees," he had said.

Her mom didn't keep anything important in the storage shed. She kept boxes of old clothes, some broken chairs, and several old issues of *Nursing Life* magazine in the shed. Rachel's mom kept saving stuff to sell at a garage sale, but they never seemed to have the sale. The stuff just kept piling up.

Rachel went inside and hung her mittens, scarf, and hat to dry on the hooks in the hallway. *If it gets much colder, I'll be wearing my mittens to bed,* she thought.

A few minutes later, Rachel heard a voice. "Rachel, I'm home!" Mrs. Henson called as she walked into the apartment.

"I'm over here, Mom," Rachel answered. Rachel ran to meet her mother in the hall. Mrs. Henson took off her heavy coat. She was wearing her new white uniform. "I don't know why they make us wear white. You can see every little spot on white," she said, scratching at a red stain. "This spot is spaghetti sauce."

Rachel made a face. "That's gross," she said.

"And these spots are grease from the fryer." Her mother sighed. "I don't know, Rachel. Maybe I wasn't cut out to be a waitress in a coffee shop."

"No, you weren't cut out to be a waitress, Mom! You're going to be a nurse." Rachel untied her mother's apron, and then she reached for the bottle of stain remover. "The coffee shop is only temporary until Daddy sends for us. Then we'll move to California, and you can go back to nursing school," said Rachel.

"Is there any mail?" Rachel's mom asked.

Rachel looked away. She didn't want to see the sad look on her mother's face when she found out that there wasn't anything but bills.

Mrs. Henson sighed, and then she emptied a small handful of coins and bills from her pocket. "I thought the tips would be better than this. People sit at the counter for hours reading the newspaper and getting free refills on their coffee. Sometimes I wonder if those people even have homes. Maybe they just sit in the coffee shop because it's warm inside, and they don't have any place else to go."

Rachel squirted a stream of blue liquid on the stain on her mom's apron. "Does the bag lady who feeds the pigeons in the park ever come into your coffee shop?" she asked her mom.

Mrs. Henson shook her head. "No, I don't

think she can afford even a cup of coffee. We should be thankful that we eat three square meals a day and have a roof over our heads." Mrs. Henson leaned against the wall and removed her rubber boots. She sighed, "Maybe I was too hard on your dad. I knew he was having a tough time at his job. Maybe if I was more understanding, he wouldn't have spent so much time with his friends."

"It's not your fault that Daddy lost his job," Rachel said. "Besides, you always say that things happen for the best. I mean, we are moving to *California*, right?" Mrs. Henson smoothed Rachel's hair.

"I've seen magazine pictures of kids playing volleyball on the beach in California during their Christmas vacation," Rachel continued. "Can you imagine any place being that warm?"

Rachel lifted the upside-down laundry basket that was covering the sink. In the sink was a large white rabbit with pink ears, eyes, and nose. Two Popsicle sticks were wrapped

11

around the rabbit's leg with a rubber band.

"Rachel, it's been six weeks since the accident," Mrs. Henson said, touching the rabbit's hurt leg. "Do you remember our agreement?"

"Yeah, I remember," answered Rachel. "I promised to put up signs to find Bunny's owner. But what kind of an owner would let Bunny get hit by a car?"

"It was an accident," Mrs. Henson reminded her.

"I don't think Bunny belongs to anyone around here," Rachel said. "I've talked to our neighbors, and I think someone must have lost her on their way through town."

"How many people in the neighborhood have you talked to?"

"Well, I've only talked to Mrs. Jaeckel." Rachel knew that Freddie Fantastic would never share an apartment with a rabbit.

"I don't think it's Mrs. Jaeckel's rabbit," said Mrs. Henson.

"Maybe Bunny needs a physical therapy

13

program to make her leg stronger." Rachel was trying to change the subject.

"Have you been reading my *Nursing Life* magazines?" Mrs. Henson asked.

"No, I'll leave the nursing to you, Mom," Rachel said. "I just thought that Bunny should be in perfect shape before we return her to her owner."

Mrs. Henson once saved a kitten's life by feeding it milk and raw eggs from an eye dropper. Another time she nursed a blackbird with a broken wing back to health. Mrs. Henson needed only two more semesters in junior college, and she could have gone to nursing school. She dropped out when they moved into the apartment, and she had planned to go back to school as soon as they got settled. Then Mr. Henson lost his job, and Rachel's mom had to quit school and go to work.

"Bunny's owner must really miss her a lot," Mrs. Henson said. "We wouldn't be very good neighbors if we didn't try to find her family."

Rachel lifted Bunny from the sink and held her close. Bunny was Rachel's best friend. Rachel could tell Bunny anything, and Bunny always listened. Bunny never made fun of Rachel like the Snob Squad at school did. Bunny didn't care what clothes Rachel wore. And Rachel never made fun of Bunny, no matter how many times she stepped in her water dish.

"Tomorrow, when you come home from school," Mrs. Henson continued, "I want you to make some cardboard signs to help us look for Bunny's owner. We'll tack them to tele- phone poles."

"Tomorrow?" Rachel's voice cracked.

Rachel buried her face in Bunny's soft coat. She couldn't stand the thought of giving up Bunny tomorrow, or ever.

Two

"RACHEL! Rachel! Are you ready for school yet? It's getting late. Let's go."

Rachel heard her mother calling. She was sitting on her bedroom floor, with an old coffee can. Rachel piled quarters next to the stacks of dimes and nickels. "I have $92.75," she said. "When I have $100, Bunny, I'm going to open a savings account in a bank. They'll pay me to keep my money in their vault. They call it interest."

Bunny hopped across the floor, stopping to sniff Rachel's fuzzy white slippers. Rachel laughed. "Hey, silly, those are my slippers, not rabbits!" She stroked Bunny's fur. "I'll make a special pile of money for you, Bunny," she continued, "so we can buy carrots and lettuce

17

for you. Bunny's money," she added, laughing.

Rachel kept a journal in the top drawer of her dresser. The first section was titled Freddie's Cat Box. The income column listed each 50-cent deposit.

The second section was titled Spring Flowers. Next month Rachel was planning to buy flower seeds and a box of small paper cups. She would enter that amount in the expense column. She was planning to plant one seed in each cup. Then she would put the cups on the windowsill, so the seeds would get sunlight to help them grow. If Rachel sold the flowers for 20 cents per cup, she might make as much as five or six dollars.

"Rachel?" Mrs. Henson called again. "Come on. You're going to be late."

"I'm coming, Mom."

Rachel kept her coffee can in the bottom of an old cardboard box in her room. The box was filled with odds and ends that she'd collected from behind the apartment buildings. She didn't think a burglar would empty a trash-filled old box looking for money.

She pulled a tattered old rug out from underneath her bed. She set Bunny's food and water dishes on the rug. Then she unfolded a newspaper and spread it out in the corner. Bunny was already housebroken when they found her.

"Do you ever think about your other family?" Rachel asked Bunny.

Rachel wondered if Bunny missed her old family as much as she missed her father.

"Have you made your lunch?" Mrs. Henson called again.

Rachel yanked on her knee socks. They covered her knees for a moment, and then they slid below her knobby knees. Some of the kids called her String Bean Legs. Rachel didn't like being the tallest kid in her fifth-grade class. String Bean Legs wasn't as bad as what the Snob Squad called her, though.

Rachel stopped to kiss Bunny on the nose. "Have a hoppy day," she said.

She'd crossed out the *A* in *Happy* on her Have a Happy Day poster, and she had written in an *O*. Then the poster on the wall above Rachel's bed read Have a Hoppy Day.

Rachel walked into the kitchen and looked into the refrigerator. A leftover baked potato shared the top rack with some macaroni and cheese and a carton of eggs. Below that were jars of peanut butter and jelly.

"Mom," Rachel said, "I'm tired of peanut butter."

Mrs. Henson sipped the last drop of coffee and put her cup in the sink. "Maybe we can get something else when my tips get better," she said.

"I bet I can find coupons for ham," Rachel said. "Where do you find coupons, anyway?"

"You can find them inside newspapers and magazines," Mrs. Henson answered.

"Then I'll check the garbage bin the next

time I dump Freddie's box," Rachel said.

"I don't want you poking through people's trash like a bag lady," Mrs. Henson said, stepping in front of the refrigerator. She removed a bag from the vegetable bin. "I was saving this for tonight's dinner, but maybe you'd rather have it in your lunch. The cook at work made too many."

Rachel looked into the bag. "Boy," she said, "this is a lot better than peanut butter."

Rachel pulled out four crispy pieces of chicken. "We'll split them. You can have two, and I'll have two," she said.

"Why don't you take them all, Rachel," Mrs. Henson said. "I get a free meal during my shift at the coffee shop."

Rachel sometimes wished that she could have expensive snacks in her lunch like some of the other kids had. But she had more important plans for the money that she was saving in the coffee can. She was planning to spend that money on her college education.

It had been three days since Mrs. Henson had mentioned making posters for Bunny. Rachel hoped that she had forgotten. But Mrs. Henson had remembered. She said sternly, "Today, I want you to make the signs to find Bunny's owner. Maybe we'll have time to hang them up today."

Maybe I can write the signs with invisible ink, thought Rachel. "What if no one calls?"

"We won't find out if anyone will call until we put up the signs, will we?" asked Rachel's mother.

Hmm, thought Rachel, *that's the way mothers always think.* Rachel stared out the window. A pickup truck clanked into the parking lot of the apartments in the next building. It was loaded with furniture, and a bicycle was tied onto the top. *I hope they have a kid in the fifth grade*, Rachel thought.

Rachel had a best friend last year in the fourth grade. Kristie Beal lived in apartment 312-D on the other side of the apartments where Rachel and her mother lived.

After Kristie moved to New Jersey, Rachel was so upset that she didn't want to get out of bed for two days. They said good-bye in the middle of the street and promised to write to each other every day. And they did write for awhile. But then they only wrote once a week, and then only once a month. Now Rachel sometimes had a hard time remembering what Kristie looked like.

Mrs. Henson stirred a teaspooon of instant coffee into a mug of hot water.

"Hey, Mom, did you know that everyone in California is rich?" Rachel went on.

Mrs. Henson laughed and asked, "Where do you hear these things?" She walked over to the window where Rachel was standing. They both looked out at the people unloading boxes from the truck. The people pulled the bicycle off the truck and put it on the sidewalk.

Then Rachel noticed a kid down the street balancing on a fire hydrant. The kid was almost hidden under a navy blue coat. A wool cap was pulled down over the kid's eyebrows. It was impossible to tell whether it was a boy or a girl. The kid was carrying what looked like a bundle of papers.

"That kid looks too short to be in the fifth grade," Rachel said, disappointed.

"Why don't you stop on your way to school and introduce yourself?"

"It might be a boy, Mom."

"So?"

Rachel wondered how many years it had been since her mom was in the fifth grade. "Boys collect beetles and put them inside your coat pockets during recess," explained Rachel. "They chew with their mouths open. They spit sandwich parts when they talk. They blow bubbles in their milk cartons. I could go on forever."

Mrs. Henson kissed her daughter on the cheek. "Don't forget to lock the front door, and put the key in its hiding place."

"I won't," Rachel said. "And don't work too hard, Mom."

Rachel put on her hat, mittens, and scarf. Her coat covered everything except the hair on her knobby knees. *Maybe the hair on my legs will freeze*, she thought. *Then I can break it off like icicles*.

Rachel liked a boy once for three and a half weeks. His name was Benjamin Field. She knew that he liked her, too, because he tripped her in the hall at school. When she dropped her books, Benjamin had helped her pick them up. For three and a half weeks she thought about Benjamin every night before she went to sleep. And then Benjamin started to trip someone else.

Rachel stopped at her bedroom door to say good-bye to Bunny. "Don't worry," she said. "I'll leave my crayons and marking pens at school. I can't make a sign without marking pens, can I?"

Bunny twitched her nose.

25

Rachel scratched Bunny between her floopy ears. "Maybe Mom will bring you a doggie bag—I mean, a bunny bag—when she comes home. She might even bring home some leftover salad stuff."

The morning air nipped the back of Rachel's throat, and her tennis shoes stuck to the frost on the walkway.

"Hey!" someone called.

The kid next door was walking on the curb like a tightrope.

"Hey, yourself," she replied.

"Do you live around here?"

"I live in apartment 102-A," she said.

"My name's Jerry," the kid said. "What's yours?"

Rachel still couldn't figure out if the kid was a girl or a boy. The name Jerry could belong to either a boy or a girl. "I'm Rachel Henson," she answered.

Then Jerry jumped off the curb and splashed into the muddy gutter. *Only a boy would splash in a gutter on purpose* , Rachel thought.

"I'm going to Francis Parkman Elementary," he said. "I'll be in Mrs. Patterson's fifth-grade class."

"She's my teacher too. You'll be in my class. Mrs. Patterson's okay, unless she catches you putting stuff in the girls' coat pockets," Rachel said.

"What kind of stuff?"

"I mean things like beetles," Rachel said. "Mrs. Patterson hates bugs."

Rachel noticed that the flag on her mailbox was up. She opened the mailbox while Jerry skipped across the driveway.

"That's weird," Rachel said. "The mail never comes this early. And, look at this. It's a postcard from New York City."

"What's so weird about that?" Jerry asked.

Rachel turned to face her new neighbor. She read the scribbled handwriting on the post-card. "What's weird about it is it's addressed

27

to Doris somebody. But somebody scratched out her name and wrote, 'Rachel Henson.' "

"They were probably trying to save postage," said Jerry.

"But look at the date," Rachel said. "It was postmarked October 9, 1972. That was before I was born!"

Jerry pulled his cap tightly over his ears and stuck his head inside the mailbox. "There's something else in here." He pulled out a limp orange carrot that was turning brown. "What's this? I bet someone's playing a joke on you," he said.

Rachel looked at the carrot and wondered if it was meant for Bunny.

"Weird, weird, weird. Who would want to play a trick on me?" she asked. "And why?"

Three

A S they were standing by the mailbox an elderly woman came out of the apartment building.

"Good morning, Mrs. Jaeckel," Rachel said. "Is it time to dump Freddie's box?"

Mrs. Jaeckel was bundled up to protect herself from the chilly morning. She held a copy of the *Daily Tribune* under her arm. "No, the box is fine for another couple of days." Then Mrs. Jaeckel said, "My goodness, Rachel, you look nice this morning."

Rachel didn't think she looked so nice. She looked down at her coat. It used to belong to her cousin, Norma Louise, and it hung down almost to Rachel's knees. Rachel thought that the coat was as stupid-looking as Norma Louise, who still stuck olives on her fingers even though she was 14 years old. All the pants in Rachel's closet were too short. When she wore them to school, the kids teased her. Monique Evans, a leader of the Snob Squad always asked, "What's the matter, Rachel? Are you expecting a flood?"

Mrs. Jaeckel started to turn onto the path leading to her apartment, and then she stopped. "Rachel, I'm expecting my sister for a visit. I've told her all about you and Bunny. She's looking forward to meeting both of you."

"I'm looking forward to meeting her, too," Rachel said politely.

"You'll have to be patient with her, though." Mrs. Jaeckel tapped her forehead. "Her mind isn't as good as it used to be."

Rachel remembered Jerry, who was standing nearby. "Um, Mrs. Jaeckel, this is Jerry. He just moved in."

"Hi," said Jerry.

"Hello, Jerry," answered Mrs. Jaeckel.

Jerry was looking back toward his apartment. His mother stood in the doorway. A wide-eyed little boy peeked out from behind her skirt. "Make sure you wear your mittens at recess!" Jerry's mother called.

"We aren't living at the North Pole!" Jerry yelled to his mother, and then he turned to Rachel. "Don't mothers worry about the littlest things?"

The school bus stopped at the curb, and Rachel waved good-bye to Mrs. Jaeckel. She climbed into the bus and walked down the slippery aisle. Pieces of ice had fallen off everyone's boots and had melted into a slushy mess. She thumped the back of each seat with her fingers. "Five, six, seven," she counted, before settling in the eighth row.

Jerry plopped down in the seat behind the driver. "You can't sit there!" Rachel shouted.

Jerry didn't turn around to answer Rachel. Instead, he looked at her reflection in the mirror above the driver's head. "Why not? I like to see where I'm going."

"Okay, but don't say I didn't warn you," Rachel called back. Rachel took off her hat and shook out her hair. It was long and thin— just like her legs.

"You're not allowed to chew gum on the bus," the driver said to Jerry.

There were more rules on the bus than in Mrs. Patterson's classroom. For instance, there was an invisible seating chart, and the Snob Squad always sat in the first row. The rest of the fifth grade followed, and then there were the fourth and third grades. Rachel sat between the third grade and the second grade.

Rachel thought back to the first day she rode the bus to school. She was sitting in the first seat, where Jerry was sitting now. Pamela Tucker had grabbed Rachel's lunch bag and started to make fun of what was in it. Pamela and Monique had taken out her jelly sandwich and tossed it around the bus. The last

Rachel saw of her sandwich was when Pamela threw it out the window and it landed on a dump truck. Rachel had been sitting eight rows back on the school bus ever since.

The bus slowed to its next stop. Monique and Pamela were standing on the corner. Monique was wearing her new knit hat and matching knit gloves. Monique's legs stuck out from under her coat, and Rachel could see that her socks matched her outfit.

Monique's father owned a shoe store, so she had a different pair of socks for every outfit. And she had a million pairs of shoes. At least that's how it seemed to Rachel.

None of Rachel's clothes were color-coordinated. Everything was handed down to her from her mother's friends and their children, or from relatives like Norma Louise. Most of her skirts were too short. Her coat was too big. And her knee socks were full of holes.

Monique got on the bus, stopping in front of Jerry. "Who are you?" she asked in a snobby

tone. "And what are you doing in my seat?"

Pamela stared at Jerry. "I bet he's from the apartment project," she said.

"Is that right?" Monique asked. "Are you neighbors with Rummage Sale Rachel?" She shot a mean look in Rachel's direction.

Rachel sunk lower in her seat.

"Take your seats," the driver said. "We have to get moving."

Monique didn't move an inch. "But he's sitting in my seat," she said stubbornly. "And I get motion sickness if I sit anywhere else. Do you want me to throw up all over the bus?"

Jerry stood up and walked back to the eighth row. "Where I come from," he said, sitting next to Rachel, "they don't have no girl bullies."

"*Any* girl bullies," Rachel corrected him.

"That's right."

Rachel told Jerry about Robert Cantu, Monique Evans' boyfriend. He was the fourth-grade bully last year. He threw hopscotch markers over the fence, and he stole milk money from first graders. His mother must have thought he was a bully, too, because she sent him to military school. The day that Robert left for his new school, Monique tied all the jump ropes into a giant knot. "And she's been the class bully ever since," said Rachel

"There was a bully at my last school," Jerry said. "Do you know what I did? I killed him with kindness."

"You killed him with what?"

"I killed him with kindness," Jerry repeated. "He was always making fun of me because I'm short. Do you want to hear what I did to him?"

Rachel nodded.

"I cut flowers from my neighbor's yard and had my baby-sitter write him a love note so that he wouldn't recognize my handwriting. The note was real mushy. I put the flowers and the note on his desk before school one morning. Every kid in the class saw the note before Hank did. Then everyone started to call him Flower Power, because his last name was Powers. Boy, Flower Power never called me Short Stuff after that." Jerry laughed, and then he turned serious. "The doctor says I should start growing anytime."

"Someone stuck a wad of gum under my seat!" Monique cried. "And it's all over my notebook!"

"Sometimes you have to make sacrifices," Jerry said with a twinkle in his eye. "That was my last piece of buble gum."

Rachel stuffed her scarf in her mouth to keep from laughing.

The bus bounced down two streets and around a corner. "Hey, Rachel," said Jerry. "What do you think about starting a club? Is one of those storage sheds big enough for a clubhouse if we cleaned it out first?"

"There's a lot of room in those sheds," Rachel said. "I bet a person could even live in one of those storage sheds."

The bus turned into the school parking lot. Rachel walked with Jerry to their classroom.

The whole time they walked through the hall, Jerry told Rachel all about how he played the trick on the bully at his old school.

* * * * *

"Class!" Mrs. Patterson called for attention.

"We have a new student. I'd like to introduce Jerry Welch."

"Is that *B* for Belch?" Pamela whispered.

"Welch," Mrs. Patterson said. "With a *W*. Pamela, would you pass back yesterday's math tests?"

Rachel was pleased with her score of 98 on the test. Math was one of Rachel's best subjects. She got a lot of practice on it when she counted the money in her coffee can.

Monique pounded her desk. "Who graded my paper?" she demanded. "There are red marks all over it."

"Is something wrong?" Mrs. Patterson asked.

"Somebody gave me a *C+*," Monique said.

"And every one of my answers is right, Mrs. Patterson. You can check them yourself."

"Who corrected Monique's test?" asked Mrs. Patterson.

Rachel felt like her collar was shrinking. "I did. She didn't show her work," Rachel said.

"I can't hear you, Rachel," Mrs. Patterson said. "Can you speak up?"

"What's the matter, Rachel?" Pamela asked. "Do you have a toad in your throat?"

Jerry was the only kid in the class who didn't giggle. He was writing something on a piece of paper.

"Class, be quiet please," Mrs. Patterson said, clapping her hands to get their attention. "Rachel?" Mrs. Patterson called.

Rachel cleared her throat. "The answers were right, Mrs. Patterson. But she didn't show her work."

"So what?" Monique shrieked.

"The instructions were very clear, Monique," Mrs. Patterson said. "Showing your work is as important as having the correct answer."

Monique shot Rachel a nasty look. "You'll be sorry for this, Rummage Sale Rachel."

"Monique, that will be enough of that," Mrs. Patterson said.

At that moment, Rachel just wanted to be hidden in her bed with the covers pulled over her head, hugging Bunny.

Mrs. Patterson took a set of keys from her desk and unlocked a cupboard door. No one understood why she locked up the books. No kid would want to steal a book. *If she should lock anything up, it should be the recess equipment,* Rachel thought. *A kid might want to borrow some of that stuff for a few days.*

"I have an announcement to make," Mrs. Patterson said. "We've been invited to visit MacArthur Middle School. They're having a welcome assembly, and we'll be given a special tour with the other fifth graders in the district."

"When are we doing that?" someone asked

"We'll go next week," Mrs. Patterson replied.

"But I don't have a thing to wear," Monique said.

"We'll have to go to the mall," Pamela added, "and buy something new."

Rachel made a face and rolled her eyes.

"Settle down, class," she said. "We'll talk more about this later. Now, I'd like you to open up your spelling workbooks."

Rachel unfolded the paper that Jerry put on her desk. The letters were pressed extra hard into the paper. "Why do you let them talk to you like that?" the note asked.

Rachel knew what Jerry meant. She didn't like the names they called her, either. But what could she do about it? If she said something, it would only make matters worse. *Ignore it, and maybe it'll go away.* What else could Rachel do?

Four

THE lunch bell rang, and everyone rushed to the coat closet. Rachel took her lunch bag out of her backpack, and then she moved out of the way.

Jerry followed Rachel out the door. "Do you want to sit together?" he asked as they walked to the cafeteria.

Something told Rachel that Jerry's newspaper was not wrapped around a roast beef sandwich. "I brought chicken," she said. "Do you want to share?"

"Sure," answered Jerry.

"Not too many kids buy hot lunches," explained Rachel. "Fish sticks and mixed vegetables is enough to make anyone gag." Jerry stuck out his tongue and made a gagging sound.

Rachel and Jerry found an empty table near the drinking fountain. Jerry straddled the bench, and then he ripped into his bundle. Rachel's mouth watered when she saw the thick hunk of chocolate cake with gooey icing and colorful sprinkles on it.

"The cake was a going-away present from the old neighborhood," Jerry explained.

Jerry pulled the cake in two and set half on Rachel's napkin. Rachel then put two drumsticks next to Jerry's piece of cake. "Your mom lets you have cake for lunch?" she asked. "Doesn't she make you eat any fruit or vegetables?"

"Mom's busy with my little brother in the mornings, so I make my own lunch," Jerry said, biting into a drumstick. "So, what do you think about starting a club?"

Rachel was letting the frosting melt on her tongue. "Sounds okay to me," she said.

"We'll need a clubhouse," he went on. "What do you think about using one of those storage sheds? Or maybe we could find a tree somewhere for our clubhouse."

"There aren't very many trees in our neighborhood," said Rachel.

Jerry spent the rest of the lunch hour describing the clubhouses in his old neighborhood. He said that some of the clubhouses were up in trees with steps nailed to the trunk. Others were hidden under houses with crawl spaces beneath floorboards. The best clubhouse was built out of fruit and vegetable crates with old blankets tacked on as room dividers.

Mrs. Patterson's class returned after lunch. Everyone got excited when they saw that the film projector was set up. Even though the label on the film box said *Presidents of our Time*, watching a movie was still better than spending the afternoon with a spelling or science book. Besides, with the lights turned off, they could pass notes without getting caught.

Rachel didn't spend that time writing notes, though. Instead, she drew pictures of what she thought a fort should look like. She even made a list of the things she'd keep there. There would have to be food and water. A storm might hit, and who knows how long she'd be stuck there? She would need pen and paper for writing down official rules and secrets—and thoughts. *A fort should be a place where a kid can go to just think and be by herself,* decided Rachel.

Mrs. Patterson flipped the lights on only a moment before the last bell rang. Rachel wadded her pictures into balls and dropped them in the trash can on her way to the coat closet. Jerry was still talking about his old forts as they walked across the playground to their bus.

Rachel stared through the grimy bus window at the passing mail boxes and their little red flags. The flags were in the down position, so Rachel knew that the mail had been delivered.

"We dug a hole in the dirt floor," Jerry was saying when the bus doors opened at their stop. "That's where we buried our safe, a shoe box full of club secrets."

Rachel bounced down the steps, and she ran toward the mailbox.

"What's the hurry?" he asked.

"Mr. Martin already delivered the mail," explained Rachel.

"So?"

Rachel stopped in front of her mailbox. "So, maybe there's a letter in the box."

"Are you expecting something special, like another postcard from New York?" Jerry asked.

"No, I'm not waiting for anything special," said Rachel.

"The only time I ever get mail is on my birthday. It isn't your birthday, is it?" asked Jerry.

Some things, thought Rachel, *just weren't anybody else's business.* "No, it's not my birthday," she said.

Jerry stuck his hands deep into his pockets and shivered. "We'd freeze to death in an outside fort," he said. "What we need is a place with walls."

Rachel opened the mailbox and removed a thin stack of letters. She counted three envelopes, but there wasn't anything from California. Telling her mother that there was nothing but bills made the inside of Rachel's stomach itch.

"Do you have any ideas?" Jerry asked.

"Huh?"

"Do you have any ideas about our clubhouse?" Jerry paused to kick a twig in the gutter. "Let's use a storage shed. Ours is full of moving boxes. What about yours?"

Rachel stuffed the envelopes into her coat pocket. "There's just some old junk in it," she said. "We could probably stack most of it in the corner. I'll have to ask Mom, though."

Jerry walked to the row of storage sheds underneath the carport. Some had locks on the door, and some didn't. All had warped doors, chipped paint, and rusty hinges.

"Rachel," Jerry groaned. "You don't understand. You can't ask a parent about having a fort. A fort isn't any good unless it's a secret. Maybe we'd better make a pact right now not to tell anyone about anything that happens in our clubhouse. Cross your heart, and repeat after me."

Reluctantly, Rachel crossed her heart.

"Anything that we talk about in the storage shed stays in the storage shed," he said.

Rachel repeated his words.

"And we'll keep this pact until death do us part," Jerry continued.

Rachel thought he was going to add "Amen," but he didn't.

"Now, which one is your shed?" he asked.

Rachel pointed to the door marked 101-A.

It crackled when Jerry yanked on the rusty handle. Rachel knew that there would be a mess inside, especially with the wind blowing as hard as it had been for the last few weeks. And she figured that there would be lots of cobwebs, too. *There might even be giant bugs in there*, she thought. The stacks of *Nursing Life* magazines would be covered with thick layers of dust.

"Shouldn't we wait until we have a flashlight?" Rachel asked.

Jerry crouched through the doorway. "Hey, I thought dogs weren't allowed in these apartments."

"They're not," she said, stepping through the doorway.

Jerry pointed to the inside of the storage shed. "Then what's this?" he said.

Rachel stared without blinking until her eyes adjusted to the light. The cement floor was cleaner than a fresh flake of snow. *This couldn't be our storage shed*, Rachel thought.

We must have opened the wrong door. Then Rachel noticed the stacks of *Nursing Life* magazines were set neatly against the back wall.

"You can tell me if you're hiding a dog," Jerry said. "I won't tell."

Rachel fingered the edge of an old quilt that was folded into a square bundle. Then she picked up a pillow, and feathers fell out of the open seam. She'd never seen either one of them before.

"Is that where the dog sleeps?" asked Jerry.

"You ask more questions than any other human being on earth," Rachel said. "And I told you I'm not hiding a dog in here. I think we should find some other place to build a fort. This place gives me the creeps."

"Rachel?" Mrs. Henson called just then. "Are you out there?"

"I have to go," Rachel said. "We'll look for another place tomorrow, okay?"

"Are you sure you're not hiding a dog?"

"Oh, brother," Rachel said, and left for home.

Mrs. Henson was sitting in the best chair. Her feet were soaking in a roasting pan filled with hot water and Epsom salts. But it was her eyes that told Rachel it had been a long, hard day. And it was her eyes that asked the question, *Any mail?*

Maybe tomorrow Rachel would let her mother get the mail. Then Rachel wouldn't be the one bringing bad news. And if it was good news, then she'd let her mother be happy about it first. Rachel stood behind the chair and massaged her mother's shoulders. The muscles felt like a mass of rubber bands ready to snap. She removed the envelopes from her pocket and handed them over her mother's shoulder. Mrs. Henson studied each return address for a moment. Then she let out a sigh that lasted so long Rachel was afraid she'd run out of breath.

"Mr. Madison stopped by. I guess we're a little late on our rent," said Rachel's mother

in a tired voice. Then she changed the subject. "Did you make the signs to find Bunny's
owner?" she asked Rachel.

"My marking pens are at school," Rachel
said.

Her mother took a black grease pencil from
the pocket of her uniform. "This should work,"
she said. "Let's get started right after dinner."

"I don't know, Mom. I have an awful lot of
homework," said Rachel.

Mrs. Henson reached up and patted Rachel's
hand. "Putting it off won't make it any easier.
Sometimes it's better to face unpleasant
things and get them over with." Then she
smiled and slowly shook her head. "I guess
I'm talking to myself as much as I'm talking
to you."

*Did Mom's "talking to herself" mean the visit
with Mr. Madison was bad news? Was he going
to make them leave because they were late with
their rent?* wondered Rachel. She wasn't

going to ask the questions that were on her mind because she didn't want to hear the answers.

Mrs. Henson wriggled her toes in the water.

Maybe I'll switch the last two numbers of our telephone number on the sign, Rachel thought. *Or, maybe I'll tack the signs upside down and backward on the telephone poles so people can't read them.*

Then Rachel remembered the blanket and pillow Jerry found in the shed. *Why couldn't Bunny live in the storage shed? No one would ever find out. I could play with Bunny every day after school. Maybe I could even sneak Bunny into my room at night,* thought Rachel.

"Guess what I brought home tonight?" Mrs. Henson asked.

"More leftovers?"

"Short ribs," Rachel's mom said. "Scrub a couple of potatoes."

Rachel grabbed the laundry basket and then

hurried to her room. "Hey, fuzzy wuzzy," she said, picking up Bunny. "Would you like a salad for dinner?"

Bunny nuzzled her head in Rachel's hair. "Hey! That tickles!"

Rachel set Bunny inside the laundry basket and put the basket on the kitchen counter. Then Rachel took two potatoes out of the cupboard. *Another week and these potatoes would be growing roots,* she thought.

Rachel looked out the kitchen window and saw Jerry standing by the Henson's mailbox. Rachel turned off the hot water and wiped the steaming window with a towel.

Jerry looked around, like a burglar ready to break into a house. Then he opened the Henson's mailbox.

"Hey!" Rachel cried. "What's he think he's doing?"

"Are you talking to me?" Mrs. Henson called from the other room.

"Uhh, no, Mom."

Rachel switched off the kitchen light so that she could see better and so that Jerry wouldn't see her watching him. Maybe Jerry was the person who put the postcard and the carrot in their mailbox? Maybe he was playing a trick on her. Rachel watched closely. But Jerry didn't put anything into the mailbox. He took something out.

Five

I'M *going to find out what's going on with that Jerry,* decided Rachel the next morning.

Mrs. Henson poured milk into her bowl of cereal and stirred it. "One of the waitresses called in sick this morning," she said. "I'll be working two shifts in a row, so don't worry if I'm not home by dark."

"Did I tell you that our class is going on a tour of the middle school next week?" Rachel asked. "I was wondering if you would write a note to my teacher saying that I don't have to go?"

"You don't want to go on a Field trip?" Mrs. Henson asked.

"What's the point, Mom?" asked Rachel.

"We'll be living in California next year, and I'll never see that old middle school."

Monique and Pamela were probably planning a trip to the mall so they could buy new jeans and sweaters. And they'll get new shoes from Monique's dad's store, thought Rachel.

Rachel's best outfit was a navy blue, corduroy skirt with matching vest. It was handed down to Rachel from her mother's best friend's daughter, Jenny Sowell. Jenny had inherited it from a cousin. The hem had been lowered three times and Rachel hated the three white lines at the bottom of the skirt.

Whenever Rachel passed Justine's boutique, she stopped to look at the skirt in the window. The skirt was long enough to cover her knobby knees. But it cost $29.95, and that would take a big hunk out of her coffee-can fund. And she'd promised herself never to dip into her college money—not unless it was an emergency.

Mrs. Henson let out another one of her long

sighs. "Two shifts today," she said. "Maybe I'll make twice as many tips."

"I bet the kids in California can wear shorts and sandals to school," Rachel said, wrapping her sandwich in a piece of wax paper. "What do you think they eat for lunch?"

"I saw a restaurant review in the travel section of the newspaper," her mother said. "A chef in California was making watermelon balls and sticking them with toothpicks."

"Yeah, they probably eat a lot of fruit," Rachel said, nodding. "You have to watch your diet when you spend all year in a bathing suit."

Mrs. Henson smiled. "Do you think I should learn how to swim?"

"Yeah, and you'll have to learn how to drive, too, Mom. Nobody takes buses in California. They all have their own cars." Rachel added.

"Oh, Rachel," her mother said with a laugh. "You have the craziest ideas about what California is like. It's a lot like Illinois, only warmer."

"Maybe," said Rachel, checking the clock. It was 8:15. Then she thought about Jerry. Whatever he had taken out of the Henson mailbox last night was Henson property. And Rachel wanted it.

"I don't know, Rachel. Maybe we shouldn't be talking like this about California. Just in case something happens and we end up not going to California, I don't want you to be disappointed."

"Daddy's not going to let us down," Rachel said firmly. "His letter is probably on its way through Texas right now. And you know how big Texas is, Mom. It just takes time."

Rachel said good-bye and hurried out the door. She was happy that her mom hadn't said anything more about Bunny's signs.

"Hey, you, Jerry!" Rachel's scarf flew into her mouth as she yelled. She spit it out and demanded, "I want to talk to you!"

Jerry was sitting on the curb. The collar of his coat was pulled up, and his hat was pulled down to completely cover his hair. His nose was red, and his lips were blue from the cold. *Everyone looked the same on a cold morning,* Rachel thought. *Everyone except Pamela and Monique.*

"And *I* want to talk to *you!*" Jerry shouted back.

Rachel picked up a rock and threw it in the street. "Boy, you've got a lot of nerve, Jerry Welch, to snoop in other people's mailboxes! Don't you know that that's private property?"

"That's what I want to talk to you about," he said. "I saw someone hanging around your mailbox last night. And I thought it might be the same person who put the postcard and the carrot in your mailbox."

Rachel's anger changed to curiosity. "You saw someone at our mailbox?"

"I didn't get a good look at the person because it was too dark. It was hard to tell who or what it was," Jerry said. "I'm not even sure it was a person. It looked more like a thing."

Rachel studied Jerry's face for traces of a smile. "Is this some kind of joke?"

"I swear, Rachel. I saw it. It was big and black, and it moved like a gorilla." Jerry stood up, stuck out his arms, and shifted his weight from one foot to the other, imitating an ape. "It didn't make any sounds, though. It didn't grunt or anything," he explained.

"So what was in the mailbox?" asked Rachel.

Jerry reached inside and took out a piece of paper. "Nothing much," he said. "It was just a picture that someone drew. My kid brother could do a better job."

Rachel thought that the picture did look like a child's drawing. There were two stick figures of a boy and girl in the picture. Both were about 11 or 12 years old. The girl had long, skinny legs and long, stringy brown hair. The boy's eyes were enormous and looked like chocolate chips.

"Jerry," Rachel said quietly. "I think it's supposed to be us!"

She shivered, but not from the cold.

"What's going on, Jerry?" Rachel asked. "Somebody's watching us!"

Jerry stared at the picture.

Just then the school bus turned the corner, and Rachel and Jerry hurried to take their seats.

Rachel studied the drawing on her lap. Jerry was right. The figures looked like second-grade squiggles. But there was something odd about the drawing.

"I think this was drawn by an adult," she finally said. "Maybe the person's hand was cold and shaky."

Jerry was sitting on his knees, looking out the back window. "Rachel! Look, quick!"

Rachel turned around. A beat-up pair of boots were leaning against the Henson's storage shed. The boots' soles were caked with mud and sitting on a folded newspaper. The newspaper looked like it was supposed to be a door mat.

"Do you know what I think?" Jerry asked.

Rachel was almost afraid to ask. "What?"

"I think someone's living in your storage shed," answered Jerry slowly.

Six

RACHEL stared at the storage shed and the boots on the newspaper as the bus drove away. Then she did what she always did when she was speechless. She stuck a strand of hair in her mouth and chewed on it.

"Do you know what else?" Jerry was hanging over the back of his seat. "I think that person has been putting stuff inside your mailbox."

They watched the old boots shrink into two small brown dots as the bus pulled away. Rachel slid back into her seat. "I have a creepy feeling, Jerry. Why would anyone live in a storage shed?" she asked.

"Maybe it's someone who broke out of prison," Jerry said. "Or, maybe it's a bank robber who's hiding out after a stick-up. Or what if it's a gang of terrorists?"

The bus seat felt hard against Rachel's backbone. "The quilt and pillow cases were clues," she agreed. "And the floor in the shed has never been so clean. But I don't think any bank robber would have cleaned the place up like that."

Jerry tugged on his hat as if it were a thinking cap. "Okay, so maybe it's aliens from outer space."

"What about the stuff in the mailbox? Aliens don't draw pictures," Rachel said.

Jerry kicked at the seat in front of him. A piece of mud fell off the bottom of his boot.

"*Mothers*. They're who make you take off your muddy shoes before coming into the house."

"So you think it's a lady?" Rachel asked.

The 35-minute bus ride was filled with unanswered questions. *Who was it? What was it? What did it want? And why is it putting things in the mailbox?* They didn't even look up when Monique and Pamela got on the bus.

Rachel couldn't concentrate on school that morning. Even when her mouth was saying the Pledge of Allegiance, her mind was on the storage shed.

"You'll have 30 minutes to work on your book reports," Mrs. Patterson said. Loud moans meant that some kids still hadn't read a book.

While Rachel was trying to work on her book report, Jerry tossed a folded-up piece of paper on her desk. Rachel opened it, looking up at the teacher.

Dear Rachel,

We need code names for our club. Do you like Dr. Seek and Mr. Hide? And maybe we should make it a detective club. Our first case will be finding out who's living in your storage shed. What do you think?

Yours truly,

Dr. Seek

P.S. Maybe she's a werewolf, and she only

comes out at night!

Mrs. Patterson looked up from her desk. "Okay, class. We'll work on the book reports again tomorrow," she said. "Everyone turn to page 20 in your language book."

Rachel opened her language book, and then she added a message of her own to the bottom of Jerry's note.

Dear Dr. Seek,

No, I don't think it's a werewolf. And I don't think it's Dracula or an alien. I think it's the bag lady who lives in the park and feeds the pigeons.

Yours truly,

Mr. Hide

P.S. Maybe we should wear garlic just in case.
P.S.S. I read somehwere that garlic keeps vampires away.

Rachel and Jerry passed notes during math, spelling, history, and science. They spent the lunch hour in the cafeteria huddled in a corner. Rachel traded Jerry half of her cheese sandwich for half of his peanut butter-smeared graham crackers. *He sure brings weird lunches,* she thought.

Monique slid onto the bench across from Rachel and Jerry. "What are you guys up to?" she asked slyly.

Jerry smacked his peanut butter-covered lips. "We're tracking a werewolf."

Rachel coughed, choking on a piece of lettuce.

"Don't lie to me, Jerry," Monique snapped. "Or, I'll tell Mrs. Patterson that you spent all morning writing that note."

"If you tell, then she'll take it away," Jerry said. "Then you'll never know what it said."

Pamela stood next to her friend. "Why should we care about your dumb note?" she demanded.

Jerry looked away and shrugged shyly. Then he turned to Monique. "Because it's for you." Rachel's mouth dropped open.

Monique suddenly sounded confused. The

note is for me? Really?"

"If you like Monique, then why are you sitting with Rummage Sale Rachel?" Pamela asked.

Jerry looked down, picking the nuts out of his crunchy peanut butter. "Rachel's handwriting is neater than mine," he said, "so she's writing the note for me. But now the surprise is ruined."

"Surprise?" Monique asked. "Well, what if I pretend I don't know anything?"

You won't have to pretend, Rachel thought.

"Well, maybe..." Jerry let his voice trail off.

The Snob Squad started giggling. The two girls hurried off to the bathroom.

"Is that what you meant by killing them with kindness?" Rachel asked.

Jerry nodded.

"What about Monique's note? She'll expect something really mushy," said Rachel.

"Don't worry," Jerry said. "I'll think of something."

Seven

MONIQUE kneeled on the front seat of the bus and faced the back during the ride home. She was reading out loud Jerry's note to her. "Roses are red. Daffodils are yellow. I'd rather have rabies, than be your fellow." She folded the note and pressed it against her heart.

"So, you do like me?" Monique called back to Jerry.

"She calls that a love note?" Jerry whispered to Rachel.

"Robert Cantu spent his lunch hour shooting her with rubber bands dipped in milk," Rachel said. "That's what she liked about him."

Monique called back, "Now, don't go play-ing hard to get, Jerry. I know you're just sitting with Rummage Sale Rachel to make me jealous."

Monique turned around in her seat. She and Pamela spent the rest of the ride whis-pering and giggling.

Rachel's first after-school chore was to reset the thermostat to the 66-degree mark. She noticed that the lint from Bunny's blanket had balled up on the carpet. A thick layer of dust from the furnace had settled on the furniture. There'd be lots of time to vacuum and dust after she and Jerry had staked out the shed. Her mom wouldn't be home until late, she re-membered.

"Do you want to go outside with us and get a little fresh air, Bunny?" Rachel asked. She covered the bottom of the laundry basket with an old blanket. Then she put Bunny inside the basket and draped the blanket loosely over Bunny's head. "You'll be nice and warm in here under this blanket."

There was a box of crackers on the shelf, so Rachel filled her pocket with enough to share with Jerry. Then she cut the leaves off a stalk of celery—one of Bunny's favorite treats. The last stop was the hall closet for her father's binoculars that he'd bought to take to the horse races.

"What's in there?" Jerry asked when he saw the laundry basket that Rachel was carrying.

Rachel peeled back the blanket. "I thought our club should have a mascot."

Jerry touched Bunny's long ears. "A rabbit? A real, live rabbit?"

"Haven't you ever seen a rabbit before?"

"I've only seen a rabbit's foot," he said. "And the rest of that rabbit was dead."

Rachel quickly covered Bunny's ears. "That's disgusting."

Then Rachel told Jerry about the day that Bunny was hit by a car, and why her mom had shaved the hair off Bunny's leg. "It's easier to keep the wound clean when there is no fur around it," she explained. "We cleaned the cut with soap, and we wiped it with iodine so that it wouldn't get infected. Then we set the broken leg with a Popsicle stick and wrapped it with gauze." Rachel scratched Bunny between the ears. "I'm supposed to be making signs to find Bunny's owner. But I can't stand the thought of giving her up."

"I don't blame you," Jerry said. "And what about the saying, *finders keepers, losers weepers?* Besides, you saved Bunny's life."

"I wish Mom would see it that way," said Rachel.

Rachel and Jerry spent the next hour crouched behind the garbage bin. They never saw anything interesting, only Mrs. Jaeckel taking Freddie Fantastic for a walk.

"Mrs. Jaeckel's kind of nosy," Rachel explained. "If she doesn't see us, then no one will."

Jerry told Rachel stories about his old house.

"We didn't have a big yard," he said. "But it was big enough for my mom to grow her own vegetables. Bunny would've liked it there, with all the carrot tops sticking out of the ground. I liked it, too. I used to go out to the garden to pick green beans. Of course, more beans ended up in my stomach than in the basket."

"Mom used to grow flowers at our other house, too," Rachel said. "The roses were red, and the daffodils were yellow."

They giggled, remembering the love note.

Jerry scooted a couple of dented trash cans next to the larger bin. They were protected on three sides now. No one could see in, unless they stood really close. But it was easy to see out. All they had to do was peek through the spaces between the trash cans.

While they were waiting, Jerry told Rachel about why his family moved to the apartment complex. "We needed to be closer to the hospital," he said. "Did I tell you that my brother's got this disease called asthma?

Sometimes, when he starts coughing, it sounds like he's going to cough his head off. He gets these special shots at the hospital to help him breathe."

"It's too bad that my mom's not a nurse yet," Rachel said. "Then your brother could go next door for his shots."

"Sometimes my brother can barely get out of bed in the morning," Jerry said sadly. "I feel sorry for him."

"I guess it's sort of like being an only child, huh? I mean, since your brother can't play much," said Rachel.

"It's like being an only child and an orphan," said Jerry.

Rachel didn't understand what Jerry meant. "Don't you live with your parents?" she asked.

"Dad works the midnight shift most of the time," Jerry explained. "So, he's at work when I get up in the morning. And when I come home from school, he's asleep. And my mom's always fussing over my brother."

Then Rachel understood why Jerry sometimes felt like an orphan.

Eight

THE next day Jerry and Rachel sat in their trash-can hideout, sharing a snack with Bunny.

"I sure hope we see something today," said Rachel. Bunny crawled onto Jerry's foot and sat there. He reached over and scratched Bunny's ears, like Rachel had taught him to do.

"I could call and say that I saw Bunny's sign," Jerry said. "If I kept her at my house, you could see her anytime you wanted to."

"Thanks," Rachel said. "But I wouldn't feel right about coming over to your house. I'd feel like I was bothering your brother."

"Then what are you going to do?"

Bunny was hopping around the inside of

their trash-can fort. She sniffed the side of one trash can, then sniffed the other.

"I've got a terrific idea. I can say that someone called and picked her up, and then I'll hide her in the storage shed," said Rachel.

"Yeah, but what if someone's living there?" asked Jerry.

"There are lots of sheds," Rachel said. "Besides, no one can live in one of those things forever. Well, Bunny might be able to."

They spent the next 30 minutes playing with Bunny. Jerry tied a bunch of carrots to the handle of one of the trash cans. Bunny sat on her hind feet and nibbled the tips. Each time the wind whipped through the barricade, Rachel mentioned the weather in *sunny* California.

"As soon as we get a letter from Daddy," Rachel said, "we're going to move."

"Maybe I should start writing my dad letters," Jerry said. "I've hardly seen him since we've moved here, and we live in the same apartment!" he said, almost to himself.

Rachel lifted the binoculars, looking from mailbox to mailbox. Several flags were up, so she knew that Mr. Martin hadn't delivered the mail yet. It was another day with no news. That was 46 days without a letter from her father. *And things at school weren't any better,* thought Rachel. Monique thought that Jerry hung around Rachel because he was trying to make her jealous. And Monique was sure that Rachel was trying to steal Jerry away from her. "I'm warning you, String Bean Legs," Monique said shaking her finger at Rachel in the cafeteria. "You're going to be sorry if you don't leave my boyfriend alone."

Boyfriend! Oh, brother, Rachel thought. Monique would like anyone who liked her. And that had been especially true since Robert Cantu went to military school.

Jerry had taken the binoculars from Rachel. Then he shouted, "Rachel! It's those boots that were by the shed yesterday!"

"Well, who's wearing them?" Rachel asked impatiently. "Let me see, Jerry."

"I can't see who's wearing them," replied Jerry. "Whoever it is, they're walking behind the fence. I can only see the legs."

Rachel nudged Jerry to get him to give her the binoculars. But Jerry said, "Wait a minute, here she is! It *is* a lady. And she's carrying a bag, like you said, Rachel."

Rachel grabbed the binoculars in her excitement. After she focused, she saw an old woman walking slowly, like she was afraid that she would fall down. The woman was wearing a nice-looking coat, a fluffy wool scarf, and a matching hat.

"It's an old lady all right, but she doesn't look poor. Her coat is 10 times nicer than mine. And she's wearing a big shiny pin on her coat. Hey, Jerry," she said, handing the binoculars to him, "it looks like it's a diamond."

"It can't be a diamond," said Jerry. "Bag

ladies don't have diamonds. Hmm. You're right, Rachel. She doesn't look exactly like the lady in the park with the shopping cart."

Jerry dropped the binoculars, and they dangled around his neck. "Maybe she isn't going to the storage shed," he said. "Maybe the boots are just a coincidence."

They watched as the woman stopped in front of the Henson's mailbox.

"That's her," Rachel said first.

Jerry nodded silently.

The woman tried to shove the brown bag inside the mailbox, but it wouldn't fit.

"What do you think is in the bag?" Jerry whispered with excitement in his voice.

Then the woman took something out of the bag and put it in the mailbox. She walked to the storage shed, opened the door, and went inside. A moment later, the boots appeared outside the door.

Rachel cried, "Jerry! What are we going to do?"

"I think we should go over and introduce ourselves," Jerry said. "It would be the neighborly thing to do."

"Are you crazy? We can't talk to a stranger, a street person? Besides, how do you know she's not an ax murderer?"

"Oh, come on, Rachel. Does she look like she could even lift an ax?" asked Jerry.

"Okay, she's not an ax murderer. But still, you don't know who she is, and that makes her a stranger," answered Rachel firmly.

Jerry moved one of the trash cans aside. "She won't be a stranger after we meet her," he said. "Are you coming?"

They knocked carefully on the storage shed door. There was no answer.

"Maybe we should just open the door and go in," Jerry said after knocking several times. "She might be sick or something."

Bunny's head had been sticking out between the button holes on Rachel's coat. "No, I think she's afraid to come out. And we don't want

93

to scare her away." What Rachel meant was that *she* was getting scared. And she didn't know if she wanted to meet the woman in the shed. "Let's see what she put in the mailbox, then we can meet again first thing in the morning."

Jerry followed Rachel to the mailbox. "Okay, you bring the hot chocolate, and I'll bring soup in case she's hungry."

Rachel reached into the mailbox and took out a large bunch of carrots. The tops were still attached, and they were covered with moist dirt. *Anyone who likes rabbits this much,* she decided, *must be okay.*

Nine

MRS. Henson stood in front of the bath-room mirror, putting on her makeup. "I'm sorry I couldn't get the day off," she said to Rachel.

Rachel swished water around in her mouth and spit toothpaste into the sink. "You can't work seven days a week, Mom. No one can do that."

"Saturday is one of the coffee shop's busiest days," her mother explained. "I'll be off on Monday for sure. Maybe we can plan to do something after school."

Saturday used to be Rachel's favorite day of the week. Rachel and her mother would take the express bus downtown and go to one of the museums. Rachel especially liked the Museum of Natural History, because she could see all of the dinosaur bones on exhibit. Other times, they'd go to a puppet show in the park or watch the afternoon feeding at the zoo.

"Would you like to come into town and have lunch at the coffee shop?" Mrs. Henson asked. "You could bring your friend. What is his name?"

"Jerry," Rachel responded.

Rachel didn't want to disappoint her mother, but she and Jerry already had plans for the day.

"We make the best hamburgers," Mrs. Henson said. "They come with lots of french fries and catsup."

"I don't know, Mom," Rachel said. "I'll have to ask Jerry."

Mrs. Henson looked sideways at her daughter. "You've never turned down a hamburger and fries in your whole life, Rachel Henson. Are you sure you're feeling all right?"

Rachel looked at her reflection in the mirror, searching for an expression that didn't make her look guilty. Then she crossed her big toe over her second toe, and she crossed all her fingers. Still, it didn't seem right to tell her mother a lie.

"We sort of made plans, Mom. We're going to visit a sick friend." There, that wasn't so bad. And maybe the woman really did have a sore throat or a cold from sleeping in the shed. Rachel still wasn't sure about that.

"Call, and let me know what you decide to do, so that I won't worry," Mrs. Henson said.

"Okay, Mom."

Only moments after Mrs. Henson left for work, Jerry knocked on the door. "I made you something," he said, holding an old pillowcase. He had cut two holes in the pillow case and tied the middle in a bow. "Put your arms through the hole and the knot over your head. Then you can carry Bunny on your chest like a papoose."

97

Rachel had seen parents carry their babies in papoose-type slings. She wanted to tell Jerry that the sling was one of the nicest things anyone had ever given her. But she just said "Thanks."

Then Jerry held up a black thermos. "Here's the soup," he said. "Did you remember to make the hot chocolate?"

Rachel nodded, slipping into her coat. Then she put the knotted pillowcase over her head and set Bunny in place. Bunny's long white ears brushed against her cheeks. "That tickles." Rachel looked at Jerry with appreciation. "Bunny likes it, too."

Rachel grabbed her father's old work thermos with its coffee-stained, plastic lid. She'd gotten up extra early and filled it with hot chocolate for the old woman. As they left her house, Rachel locked the front door and wiggled the knob to make sure that the latch was secure.

When they got to the storage shed, the black

boots were in the same spot. Rachel touched Jerry's arm just as he was about to knock on the storage shed door. "Do you really think this is a good idea, Jerry?" she whispered. "I guess I'm a little scared."

"Don't worry, Rachel," he answered. "Nothing bad will happen. We're doing a good deed, remember?" Jerry tapped lightly on the door. "Uh, good morning," he called into the shed. "We brought you some soup and hot chocolate. Would you like to have something to eat?"

They stared at the door. The only sound was the wind whipping dried leaves through the carport. Rachel shivered. Then she had an idea.

"There's someone who wants to see you," Rachel said. "My rabbit, Bunny, wants to thank you for the carrots."

They stood in front of the shed a few more minutes listening to the wind. Then suddenly the door opened just a crack. Jerry and Rachel both jumped back. Rachel let out a little

cry of fear, and Jerry stumbled on a pile of newspapers. Their eyes were wide with anticipation.

Staring at them through the narrow opening in the door was an old woman's gray face. She looked as frightened as they did.

"Are you Rachel?"

Rachel jumped back again, startled. "She knows my name," she whispered to Jerry.

"Yeah," Jerry said. "She wrote it on the postcard, remember?"

"That's right," answered Rachel. "Still, it feels weird having a stranger know my name."

The woman in the shed seemed to become less afraid after she saw it was Rachel. "I don't think I've had the pleasure of being introduced to you, young man," the woman said looking at Jerry.

Jerry wiped his hand on his coat, and he held his hand out to shake her hand. "I'm Jerry Welch," he said. "And who are you?"

"It's my housekeeper's day off," the woman said. "My parlor is a bit messy, and I'm out of tea."

Jerry and Rachel looked at each other nervously. *I wonder if this woman is crazy,* thought Rachel to herself. *Maybe we ought to get out of here fast.*

But before she could say anything to Jerry, he unscrewed the lid on his thermos and poured a steaming cup of soup. As he carefully held out the cup, the woman opened the door. "It's so nice to have callers," she said. "Please, won't you both come in?"

Jerry turned to Rachel. "Come on," he said. "Let's go in before she changes her mind."

"Maybe we shouldn't go in. I think she's crazy," Rachel said in a whisper. "And she talks funny, not like any street person I've ever heard."

Rachel had heard the bag lady in the park talking to the pigeons. Her two front teeth were missing so her *s*'s made a *th* sound.

"Birdth," the bag lady would say, pointing to the sky. Then there was the man who stood on a corner and talked about the end of the world. Neither of them spoke like the woman in the shed did.

"No, I don't think she's a street person," Jerry whispered back. "And she shouldn't be living in any shed, either. We should find out who she is and where she comes from. Maybe she has a family somewhere," Jerry whispered as they stood just outside the shed.

Rachel took a carrot from her pocket and fed Bunny. *What kind of family would let a relative live in a storage shed?* Rachel wondered.

Jerry stooped in the doorway. "There isn't anyone else to help her, Rachel. Come on. She's as harmless as a pussy cat."

Rachel sighed a longer sigh than any of her mother's. "I guess you're right," she said. "I have to remember we're doing a good deed." She took a deep breath and stepped inside.

The inside of the shed hadn't changed much since they'd looked into it two days ago. The concrete floor was still clean, and the quilt was folded in a neat stack on top of the old pillow.

Rachel watched the woman sip soup. "I've been very hungry, since my cook's been on vacation. And my handyman forgot to chop wood for the fireplace," the woman said.

Jerry and Rachel watched the old woman drink the soup. She seemed very hungry, and the woman asked if she could have some more. After she finished her second cup of soup, she set the top of the thermos down and said, "I'm afraid I've lost my glasses. Would you mind reading a story from my books?"

Rachel looked around but didn't see any books, so she decided to tell her favorite story, *The Prince and the Pauper*. Even Jerry listened to the story about a prince who changed places with a poor boy. Bunny was sound asleep in the old woman's lap.

"That's a lovely story," the woman said when Rachel had finished. "Now I'll tell you a story."

The woman's eyes sparkled as she told them about a fairy princess and a toad named Croaker. Rachel realized that the woman's eyes were the same deep blue color as the stones in her ring. *Maybe they're sapphires,* Rachel thought. *They're probably not a cheap imitation, either, but real sapphires.*

"Croaker jumped through the air to save the fairy princess from the fire-breathing dragon. Croaker was then crowned King of the Croakers, and everyone lived happily ever after. The end," the woman finished her story.

"That was a neat story," Jerry said, stretching his legs.

"After all these wonderful stories," said the woman, "I think it might be time for dinner, don't you?"

Jerry and Rachel exchanged looks. They had just had breakfast.

"I've always been fond of leg of lamb, with

freshly made mint jelly," the woman said. "Of course, a standing rib roast is nice if it's cooked properly."

Rachel had never tasted lamb, and mint jelly sounded disgusting. And she didn't know what a standing roast was. The only roasts she had ever seen were laying down.

The sparkle left the woman's eyes. "I've been so hungry lately."

Jerry stood up. "Then we'll bring you something to eat," he said. "How does a juicy steak sound? And maybe you'd like a new pair of wool socks, and a real book with stories about—"

Rachel yanked on Jerry's sleeve before he made any other promises. "Have you gone crazy, Jerry Welch?"

Jerry gave Rachel a look that said *Come on. Let's go.* Rachel got to her feet, and they walked toward the door.

"I'll have all the silver polished before you return," the woman said. "And I'll take the good china down from the cupboard."

Rachel looked at Jerry and shook her head. "This is getting pretty weird, Jerry," she whispered. She then ducked through the doorway to leave. But she turned around and said, "Excuse me. Will you take care of Bunny while we're gone?" she asked. "They don't allow rabbits in the grocery store."

The woman smiled a big smile and took the rabbit. She was rocking Bunny and singing her a song when they left. Jerry looked at his watch and said, "Wow! We've been in there over two hours!"

They headed for Rachel's apartment. "I don't know," she began. "Maybe we should call the police. That lady needs help."

"No!" shouted Jerry. "We can't call the police!"

"Why not? We should file a missing persons report," said Rachel.

"Don't you watch TV?" he asked. "They'll put her in a cell and give her bread and water.

Is that what you want to happen?"

Rachel thought for a second and then said, "Most of that stuff you see on TV isn't even real. They make it up."

"Maybe. Maybe not," answered Jerry.

"And why would they lock her in a cell? They only arrest people who break the law."

Jerry said, "Well, what if they send her to one of those old folks' homes?"

Rachel sighed. "Okay, we won't call the police."

When they got to Rachel's front door, Jerry said, "How much money did you say was in your coffee fund?"

"That's college fund, not coffee fund. And I'm not spending it on dead sheep."

"I don't want you to spend your college money."

"You don't?"

Jerry shook his head. "It'll be a loan until I can pay you back."

"How are you going to pay me back if you

don't have any money?"

"We're going to sell newspaper coupons in front of the grocery store, right?" Jerry reminded her. "Come on, Rachel. There's lots of time to save for college."

Rachel unhooked the Henson's key from its secret nail. "Wouldn't you like to see the look on the old woman's face if we brought her a steak?" asked Jerry.

Rachel hadn't eaten steak since they'd moved into the apartment complex. "Yeah," she said after a while. "Maybe I would like to see the look on her face."

"We can stop at the store and pick up a few supplies." Jerry unlocked the front door. "Maybe a flashlight and a pair of long underwear, and—"

"You don't have to pay me back," Rachel said. "We'll split whatever the stuff costs, 50-50."

Rachel wanted half of the happy look on the woman's face to belong to her. Maybe it would make up for her mother's sad looks that Rachel saw each time she brought in the mail and there was no news from her dad.

Ten

JERRY stuck a fork into a thick steak and flipped it over. Grease splattered all over the Henson's stove. "How do you know when it's done?" he asked. "I've never cooked anything but hot dogs and marshmallows. And I always burn them to a crisp!"

Rachel was taking things out of the store bag. There was a pair of wool socks, a flashlight and batteries, earmuffs, and mittens. Another bag contained a brand new copy of *Swiss Family Robinson*. "I'll bet the woman feels like she's living on an island since she's all alone," Rachel said.

"She's not alone," Jerry replied. "She's got us, doesn't she?" He was drawing a line on the greasy stove with his finger.

Rachel removed the receipt from the store bag. The total was $16.48. *Swiss Family Robinson* cost $7.30. Rachel added the two receipts. That total was $23.78. *That was a lot of money out of her savings for college*, she thought.

"You know what we forgot?" Jerry asked. "We forgot paper plates, napkins, and plastic forks."

"You make it sound like she's going to be living in the shed forever," Rachel said. She put the things back in the bags. "I've been thinking. Maybe we should just call the police to see if someone's filed a missing persons report for her."

"Rachel, we already talked about this. We can't call the police. Tomorrow's Sunday. We'll have lots of time to think of something then," Jerry said.

Rachel sprinkled the steak with salt and pepper. "We wouldn't be very good friends if we didn't do everything we could to find her family."

Rachel stopped in the middle of her sentence. She was using the same words her mother had used when she talked to Rachel about finding Bunny's owner.

"I promised to call Mom at work and let her know if we were going to come into town, or not," Rachel said, picking up the telephone. "She'll worry if I don't."

Rachel looked up the number of the coffee shop and dialed. "Hang on," a man said, "and I'll get her."

"Rachel? Is that you?" her mother asked.

"Yes, Mom. I just called to say that we're not coming into town."

"Well, maybe you can come another time." Mrs. Henson sounded disappointed. "Is your friend feeling better?"

Rachel cleared her throat. "Jerry and I are on our way to see her now, Mom."

"That's nice, dear," Mrs. Henson said. "And, Rachel, I want Bunny's signs made today. Do you understand? We can't put it off any longer."

"Okay, Mom."

"Do you promise?"

Rachel swallowed hard. "I'll do my best, Mom."

They said good-bye, and Rachel hung up.

Why was everything so complicated? That's what Rachel wanted to know. Rachel thought of all the things that were making her life so complicated. Last week all she wanted was a letter from her father. Sometimes it bugged her that the kids at school teased her. But most of the time, she ignored them.

But now there was a strange woman living in her storage shed. Her new neighbor—a boy—was frying a steak on her stove. And, unless she won a scholarship, she wouldn't be going to college. And then there was Bunny. Would Bunny be happy living in the storage shed?

"Aren't you going to get that?" Jerry shouted.

"Get what?" Rachel asked.

"The door bell. Are you deaf?" he asked.

"I guess I was just daydreaming," said Rachel. The bell rang again, and it was followed by a

114

loud knocking. "Are you in there, Rachel?" It was Mr. Martin. "I think I have what you've been waiting for."

Could it be the letter from California? Rachel wondered. She had been disappointed so many times that now she was almost afraid to answer the door.

"Are you in there, Rachel?" Mr. Martin repeated. "I don't have all day."

"Do you want me to let him in?" Jerry asked.

"No," Rachel said, "I'll get it."

"I don't usually make house calls," Mr. Martin said when Rachel opened the door. "But in this case, I thought I'd bring your letter to you."

Rachel took the letter and held it against her chest. "Are you sure this is the one?"

"There's only one way to find out," Mr. Martin said. "Open it."

Open it? Rachel was afraid to *look* at it.

Jerry shut the door with his foot. "Is it the letter you've been waiting for from your dad?"

Rachel tilted the envelope away from her

115

chest to see if it was postmarked from California. It wasn't. She shook her head slowly and said, "No, Mr. Martin was wrong. This can't be from Daddy. It's from someone in Kalamazoo, MI."

"That's somewhere out west, isn't it?"

"No, MI is Missouri, I think," she said slowly. "And it isn't even addressed to me. It's addressed to Mrs. Edgar Henson. My dad's name is Edgar, but everyone calls him Ed. And I don't recognize the handwriting. It's all a mess, see?"

Jerry looked closer. "What's the return address say? It must be on the back of the envelope," he said.

Rachel turned the letter over in her hand to see who it was from.

E.P. Henson, General Delivery,
Kalamazoo, MI 48104

She shook her head slowly, and a strand of hair stuck to her mouth. She bit down hard on her hair to keep from crying. *Was it Missouri with a*

116

capital MI? wondered Rachel.

"He's probably passing through Missouri on his way to California," Jerry said. "Why don't you open it and see?"

"He didn't even make it to Texas," Rachel said sadly. "And I can't open it. It's addressed to Mom."

"Maybe we can hold it up to the light and read through the envelope. Or, we could steam it open, like they do on detective shows."

"Messing around with the mail is a federal offense," she reminded him. "Besides, opening someone else's letter isn't nice."

If the letter had been from Calfironia, Rachel admitted, she might have considered steaming it open. She'd wanted to hear from her father for so long. But now that the letter had arrived, she wasn't even excited. She felt like a balloon that had lost all of its air.

She was certain that Kalamazoo, Missouri, meant bad news.

"Maybe you should call your mom," Jerry said.

"She might want you to read it over the phone."

"Don't you ever mind your own business, Jerry Welch?" Rachel spit the words out.

Jerry stepped back, startled.

Dear Pauline, the letter might begin,

There's been a change of plans, and we're not going to California.

Or it might say,

Dear Pauline,

I'm sorry I can't help out with the rent, but...

Or worse yet, it might say,

Dear Pauline,

Maybe it's time that we get a divorce. Tell Rachel I said good-bye.

Rachel felt tears coming into her eyes. *Come on, Rachel*, she told herself. *Pull yourself together. Just don't think about it right now. We have too much to do.*

Rachel put the letter on the kitchen counter and turned to the steak. "We should put a lid on the steak, so it won't get cold when we carry it to the shed," she said. The top on the big pot was just the right size. "She'll need a fork and a knife. And I'd better take a couple of napkins. And, Jerry, open the kitchen window so the smell goes out of here. We don't want Mom to know we were cooking steak in here."

Jerry smiled. "You're starting to sound like me."

"Um, Jerry," Rachel said. "I'm sorry I yelled at you just then. I guess I'm kind of disappointed about the letter."

"That's okay," said Jerry. "Maybe it'll work out."

The old woman was sitting in the same position as before when they returned to the shed. She sat cross-legged, with the quilt draped over her lap. Bunny was sniffing around the old boxes.

"It's a fine specimen of Angora," the woman said, referring to Bunny's sleek coat. "I had an Angora cat once, and that's what we named him, Aristotle Angora."

119

Jerry made a table with an upside-down crate, and Rachel set a proper place with a knife, a fork, and a folded napkin. Rachel shivered, and this time it was not from the cold. It made her proud to share her coffee-can money with the old woman. Besides, Jerry was right. She had lots of time to earn money for college. She'd just have to work extra. That's all.

The woman cut a small bite of steak while Rachel tore pieces of lettuce and fed Bunny.

"Tell me a story," the woman said to Jerry. "Dinner theater is such fun."

"Me?" Jerry asked. "I don't know no stories."

"Any stories," Rachel corrected him from the corner. "And, yes, you do. Tell her the story about the bully in your other school, and how you killed him with kindness."

"A murder mystery?" the woman asked.

Jerry looked at Rachel, and Rachel nodded.

"Once upon a time," Jerry began slowly, "in a land far away called Chicago, there was a monster named Hank Powers. And he bullied all the little people, until one day a knight rode into the kingdom and—"

Bunny jumped into Rachel's lap, and they settled in to listen to the story. Rachel realized that she was starting to like Jerry, even if he was a boy.

Eleven

ACHEL gave the woman a name because
she didn't like calling her "the old
woman." *Angelica Aristotle Angora is a beau-
tiful name*, Rachel thought. *An 11-syllable
name would only belong to someone very
dignified.*

Mrs. Angora had only eaten one quarter of
her steak before wiping the corners of her
mouth. "Bless you," she said, folding her
napkin into a neat triangle, "for such a fine
meal."

Rachel and Jerry cleaned up the dinner
dishes and returned to the Henson's kitchen.
They were eating what was left of the steak.
"I think we should take her something hot for

breakfast," Rachel said. "I wonder if she likes oatmeal?"

Jerry cut a very large bite from his half of steak. "Do you have any catsup?"

"It's in the refrigerator."

"And what do you want to do about lunch?" Jerry smacked the bottom of the upside-down catsup bottle. "I vote for salami on rye, with lots of mustard. And we'll put dill pickles on the side. Do you have any salami?"

Rachel shook her head. "Not unless Mom brings some home from work."

"Then we'll have to make another trip to the store."

Rachel groaned. "Good-bye, college. Hello, poor farm."

Rachel cut her steak into as many pieces as she could without it looking like ground hamburger. She moved each bite around in her mouth until there was nothing left, and then she swallowed. She couldn't remember the last time she'd eaten steak. Jerry gobbled his steak down and started gnawing on the bone.

"I've been thinking," Rachel said between bites. "Why can't we make 'Found' signs and put them up around the neighborhood on telephone poles, like I was going to do for Bunny?"

"What would we say?" wondered Jerry.

"Wait a minute. I'll be right back," Rachel said and ran to her room.

She returned, carrying poster board and a box of markers. FOUND, she wrote in giant red letters, ONE WOMAN. Then she made an arrow between ONE and WOMAN, and added ELEGANT.

"We can use my telephone number since Mom's not home much," she said. "And I'll make sure I answer the phone when Mom is home."

Jerry picked up a bright blue pen. "What about her description?"

Rachel stuck the end of the pen in her mouth, thinking. "She has blue eyes. We've never seen much of her hair, though, because she's always wearing that knitted cap. But I bet it's gray, like her eyebrows."

Rachel wrote on the poster board, BLUE EYES AND GRAY HAIR, and then she added the Henson's telephone number. "You know what? Ever since I first saw Mrs. Angora," she said, "she's reminded me of someone. But I can't figure out who."

Jerry hunched over his paper and wrote "found" in very small letters. The letters were so small that no one could read them without a magnifying glass. And if it was tacked high up on a telephone pole, forget it!

"Yeah, now that you mention it," Jerry said. "She does look like someone I've seen before. Maybe it's someone on TV that she looks like."

Rachel finished her second sign and was working on her third. "Nah, I think it's more like a real person."

Jerry shrugged, writing Rachel's phone number in the lower corner of his poster. He made the six look like a nine. "The rules say

no dogs," he said. "But they don't say anything about little old ladies."

Rachel raised her eyebrows.

"Oh, don't look at me like that, Rachel," said
Jerry. "I know Mrs. Angora is a person, and
that people can't be pets."

But Rachel understood how Jerry felt about
Mrs. Angora. It was the same way she felt
about Bunny. And Rachel would miss Mrs.
Angora, too. She would especially miss the
secret notes and drawings in the mailbox, and
the gifts for Bunny.

Mrs. Angora was a special person, Rachel
decided. And special people made very special friends.

Rachel gathered the posters into a pile.
"Maybe she's just lost. I bet she has a fancy
house on the other side of town. We can take
the bus and visit her anytime we want to, or,
maybe she'll send her chauffeur to pick us
up. And she'll serve us tea in china tea cups
and some chocolate-chip cookies on a silver

platter. It'll be great."

"Do you really think so?" Jerry asked.

"Why not?"

Rachel and Jerry spent the rest of the afternoon making posters and tacking them up around the neighborhood. They put up four neatly written signs with large letters, and Jerry's two signs. Rachel only missed the nail once, smashing the safety pin on the end of her mitten.

They were standing in the middle of the street, admiring their work, when the bus from downtown turned the corner. Rachel's mother waved from a back window.

"Do you think she saw the signs?" Jerry asked.

Rachel took the nails out of her mouth and held the hammer behind her back. "I hope not."

"Rachel," Mrs. Henson said, stepping off the bus. "I'm so proud of you."

Rachel passed the hammer, behind her

back, to Jerry. "Me?" she asked.

Mrs. Henson glanced down the street at the telephone poles. "You actually put up the signs. That's what you had planned for today, isn't it? I bet you didn't really have a sick friend to visit."

Rachel didn't know what to say. Her mother had seen the signs, but she hadn't read beyond the word "Found."

"I think I hear my mom calling," Jerry said. "I'll see you tomorrow, Rachel."

Mrs. Henson rested her arm on Rachel's shoulder as they walked to the apartment. "See?" Mrs. Henson asked, unlocking the front door. "Sometimes doing something you don't want to do isn't as bad as you think it's going to be. Isn't that right?"

Rachel knew that her mother was talking about Bunny's signs, or what she thought were Bunny's signs. She wanted to tell her mother the truth, but how could she tell her without breaking her promise to Jerry to not talk to anyone about things that happened in the shed?

"I guess so," she found herself saying.

"I don't have any leftovers today," Mrs. Henson said. "But I got really good tips. Do you want to count it for me, Rachel?"

"How much do you have in your coffee can?" she went on. "Do you have $100 yet? Do you know what you can buy with a college education? You can buy choices to be whatever you want to be. You can be a nurse, or even a doctor, if that's what you want."

Mrs. Henson emptied her pockets full of change, and then she sat down. "Boy, does that ever feel good," she said, sinking into the chair. "There's nothing wrong with being a waitress, Rachel. But you should be able to decide if you want to be a waitress, and not be pushed into it."

Rachel cleared her throat. "Mom?"

"Hmm?" asked Mrs. Henson.

"The letter came," said Rachel, trying not to

sound as disappointed as she felt.

Rachel went to get the envelope postmarked Kalamazoo.

Mrs. Henson slipped her finger under the flap. "I knew it would come," she said, removing a scruffy piece of paper.

Two $20 bills fell to the floor, and Rachel picked them up. "Mom!" she shouted excitedly. "Do you know how many flowers I'd have to sell to make this much money? Read the letter. Has he already left for California?"

Rachel felt herself getting more and more excited. At least, if the news wasn't all good, she'd have her mom there to tell her that everything was going to be all right.

"How is he? Does he miss us?" Rachel hurried on. "What does it say, Mom?"

Mrs. Henson stared at the $20 bills for a long time. Then her neck disappeared into her sagging shoulders. "We needed at least $150, plus my salary, to make ends meet."

"Read the letter, Mom. Maybe he's going to

send more money. Maybe he's already sent more, and we just haven't gotten it yet.

Mrs. Henson cleared her throat, and then she read the letter out loud.

"Dear Pauline," she paused. "I got a part-time job as a janitor in a school. I hope $40 will help a little. I'll try to send more later. Yesterday I heard about a job that pays better wages at a factory not far—"

"But what about California?" Rachel cut in. "What's he say about California?"

Mrs. Henson's eyes were cloudy as she went on, "—a factory not far away. Tell Rachel that I love her and miss her a whole bunch. Love always, Ed. P.S. Things are bound to get better."

Rachel leaned wearily on the arm of the old chair. "He didn't say anything about California," she said quietly. Then after a long pause, she added, "It was all a lie, wasn't it? He just made up the whole thing."

Rachel ran into her bedroom and slammed

133

the door. The walls shook like they did the night her dad had slammed the front door and left.

Twelve

WHEN Rachel got into bed that night, she went over the day in her mind, trying to figure out what had gone wrong. But all she could remember was her father's letter, *I've heard about a better job at a factory that's not too far away...not too far away...not too far away...*

She had trouble falling asleep without Bunny to cuddle around. And when she finally did fall asleep, she dreamed that she was on the tour of the middle school. She was wearing an old T-shirt that her mother wore to clean house. It was stained with furniture polish. "Rummage Sale Rachel, Rummage Sale Rachel," Monique and Pamela sang in her dream. Everyone else laughed.

The next morning, Mrs. Henson sat on the edge of her daughter's bed. "Rachel, it's 8:30. And I have to leave for work. Wake up," she said gently. "I want to talk to you."

Rachel rolled over. "Huh?"

"Are you awake?" Her mother's voice was scratchy, as though she'd been crying. Her eyes were red. "This is important."

Thoughts bounced around Rachel's head like a million Ping-Pong balls. *Mom found out about the signs*, Rachel thought. *And she found out about Mrs. Angora living in the storage shed.*

"Mr. Madison called last night after you went to bed. He said that if we don't pay our rent by noon tomorrow, he's going to rent our apartment to someone else. I hate to ask you, Rachel, but I need a loan from your coffee can."

Rachel blinked away the last traces of sleep. "My college fund?"

"I know how much it means to you," her

mother said. "And I'll pay you back as soon as I can. But I need another $100 to pay the rent, or we'll be kicked out of the apartment."

Oh, no, thought Rachel. *She wants my money, and I've already spent some of it.* Rachel looked at her mother for a long time. She saw how red and tired her eyes were. Rachel felt tears coming into her own eyes. Finally, she figured out the right thing to do. "Sure, mom," Rachel said sadly. "You can have the money."

"We have to stick together, now more than ever," said Mrs. Henson.

Mrs. Henson took a tissue out of the pocket of her uniform and wiped her nose. The circles under her eyes were darker and deeper than usual. "I'm sorry, Rachel. I'm sorry about everything. Sometimes things just don't work out the way you want them to, no matter how hard you try. But it isn't anybody's fault. It's not your daddy's fault, or mine or yours. It's just the way it is. I wouldn't ask you for—"

Mrs. Henson was interrupted by a loud knock on the front door. *It's Jerry*, Rachel thought. *It's time to make breakfast for Mrs. Angora.* Rachel wished more than ever that Bunny was there for her to cuddle around. But Bunny now lived in the shed.

"I bet it's Mr. Madison," her mother said, turning toward the door. "He just couldn't wait until tomorrow to collect the rent."

Rachel slipped into her robe and followed her mother to the front door. But it wasn't Mr. Madison knocking. And it wasn't Jerry.

"Rachel!" Mrs. Jaeckel burst into the living room. Freddie Fantastic was under her arm, kicking his hind feet. "You found her? Oh, you found her!"

"Calm down, Mrs. Jaeckel," Mrs. Henson said. "Rachel found who?"

"I didn't even know she was missing until this morning," Mrs. Jaeckel wailed. "I called the nursing home to see why she hadn't arrived. I told you that she was coming for a

visit, didn't I, Rachel? Didn't I tell you that my sister was coming?"

Rachel nodded, confused.

"The nursing home said that they put her on a bus days ago. They gave special instructions to the bus driver, but when the bus got a flat tire, they changed drivers. Then, I don't know. Everything got all messed up." Mrs. Jaeckel was sobbing quietly now. "I saw the signs this morning when I took Freddie for his walk. And I recognized your phone number, Rachel. I'm sorry I burst in like this, but I couldn't wait to see her. Rachel, please take me to her."

And then Rachel understood. She recognized the sparkling blue eyes, the gray eyebrows, and the wrinkly smile. Now she knew why Mrs. Angora had looked so familiar.

Mrs. Angora was Mrs. Jaeckel's sister.

"Come on," Rachel said. "She's in the storage shed."

Mrs. Henson and Mrs. Jaeckel exchanged

140

confused looks. "The storage shed?" they both asked.

Rachel put on her coat over her robe, and she led the way to the carport. "Mrs. Angora?" she called, knocking lightly on the door.

"Veronica?" Mrs. Jaeckel called. "Is that you in there?"

"More company!" Mrs. Angora cried from inside the shed. "My goodness!"

The door opened, and Mrs. Angora stepped into the morning light. Mrs. Jaeckel pushed Freddie Fantastic into Rachel's arms and hugged her sister. "Veronica! Are you all right? I've been worried sick about you!" she cried.

"Why, yes, dear," Mrs. Angora answered. "Is something wrong?"

Bunny hopped out of the shed, and Mrs. Henson stooped to pick her up. She looked at Rachel, and then down at Bunny. "I think we have a few things to talk about, Rachel," she said.

Rachel took a deep breath and started at the beginning. She told her mother all about the gifts in the mail box and the boots left outside the shed door. Then she told her how she and Jerry had staked out the shed, waiting for someone to show up. She even told her mother about the trip to town, and the steak, and *Swiss Family Robinson*.

Mrs. Henson listened to the story. "I just can't believe it! Why didn't you come to me, Rachel? Why didn't you tell me about it, and ask for help?"

"It was our secret clubhouse," Rachel explained. "And we made a pact not to tell anyone about it. I crossed my heart and swore, Mom, *until death do us part*. Besides, you had enough things to worry about."

"I always have time to listen. And you know you're not supposed to talk to strangers."

Rachel listened to every word that her mom said. "But she wasn't a stranger, Mom. She knew my name."

"That doesn't matter," Mrs. Henson said. "Everyone's a stranger, unless you know *that person's* name."

When they were back inside the apartment, Mrs. Jaeckel and Mrs. Angora sat on the Henson's couch while Mrs. Henson telephoned the hospital emergency room. "They said she'll need a complete check-up after being exposed to such extreme temperatures," Mrs. Henson explained.

"I can't believe they put you on a bus all by yourself," Mrs. Jaeckel went on. "They didn't even call me to make sure that someone would be able to meet you. There will be no more nursing homes for you, Veronica. From now on, your home is with me."

Rachel added, smiling, "And with Freddie Fantastic."

The ambulance cruised down the street between the rows of apartment buildings and parked in the Henson's carport. The lights were flashing, but the siren was turned off.

143

Two paramedics in crisp, white uniforms emerged from the front cab. They opened the rear double doors and let down a stretcher on wheels.

"What's going on?" Jerry raced out of his apartment. "I thought they were here for my brother."

Rachel and Jerry watched as the paramedics strapped Mrs. Angora onto the stretcher. "It's just a safety precaution," they explained. Then they lifted the stretcher into the back of the ambulance.

Mrs. Jaeckel sat next to her sister in the ambulance. "And we'll turn my sewing room into your bedroom," Rachel heard Mrs. Jaeckel say before the doors to the ambulance shut.

Rachel's mother sat up front between the two paramedics. She went along to the hospital to answer questions and to help fill out forms. Her boss had given her the day off after she had called in and explained the situation.

Rachel told Jerry about everything that had

happened. "And we'll be able to visit Mrs. Angora anytime we want to," Rachel continued. "It's a happy ending just like the story that she told us about Croaker."

They watched the ambulance until it was a tiny dot in the distance.

"I guess we'll have to find a new clubhouse," Jerry said. "Do you have any ideas?"

Rachel smiled. It was nice to have a friend—someone you could count on. Even if he was a boy.

Thirteen

RACHEL flipped through the hangers in her closet. "Today's the tour of the middle school," she said to Bunny. "What do you think I should wear?"

Bunny stuck her nose under the pile of clothes lying on the closet floor and wiggled her tail.

"Should I wear pants? No, they're all too short."

Rachel would have to wear a skirt on the tour of the middle school. A faded old one that had been handed down to her from Louise Sowell, or some other cousin.

"I bet the kids in college don't make fun of what the other kids wear. I bet they're too busy study-ing to be doctors and lawyers to notice what

147

everyone else is wearing," Rachel said to Bunny.

Rachel pulled the navy blue, corduroy skirt off of its hanger and took it into the bathroom. She used her mother's navy blue eye shadow to color the white line from the last time the hem had been let down. Rachel heard her mother's voice. "Rachel, aren't you ever coming out of that bathroom? I need to talk to you before I go to work."

Rachel shut the bathroom drawer and followed the smell of burned bread to the kitchen. A piece of overdone toast popped out of the toaster, and Mrs. Henson scraped the black crumbs into the sink with a knife. She was dressed in her white uniform, ready for another day at the coffee shop.

Rachel poured some cereal into a bowl and took it to the table. Rachel's mother sat down with her coffee and toast. "Do you remember what you said when I asked if I could borrow your coffee-can money to pay the rent?" she asked and then took a sip of her coffee.

Rachel thought a moment and said, "You

mean about us having to stick together, now more than ever?"

"That's right," her mother answered. "Well, Rachel, I think we have to face the fact that your dad might be staying in Michigan for a while, and we might have to stay here."

"Michigan?" asked Rachel. "I thought that Kalamazoo, MI, was in Missouri, on the way to California."

Mrs. Henson shook her head, "No, dear, it's Michigan. It's where Dad's cousins live. What I want you to know is that it looks like it might be the two of us for a while. But we'll manage, won't we, Rachel?"

Rachel looked out the kitchen window. *There are still no buds on the trees*, she thought. *Won't it ever be spring?*

"Sure, Mom," said Rachel with a sigh. "We'll manage if we stick together." She and her mother hugged for a long time, until Mrs. Henson said, "Well, finish your breakfast. It's getting late. Let's talk about this more later."

Rachel gulped down her cereal and put her bowl in the sink. Her mother said, "Rachel, about Bunny—"

"I'm out of poster board, Mom. We used it all," said Rachel.

Mrs. Henson smiled and said, "What I was going to say was that maybe it would be all right if we keep Bunny after all. You might want to get Jerry to help you build a cage. Mrs. Jaeckel's sister found a new home, where she really belongs. Maybe Bunny can find a new home too, with us."

"Oh, Mom, that's fantastic. Thank you. Bunny thanks you. I'll talk to Jerry today."

"But, Rachel, if we see any signs for a lost rabbit, we'll have to give her back to her owner," said Mrs. Henson.

Rachel let out a shriek of happiness and ran to her room to cuddle Bunny. She smothered Bunny with kisses.

"Rachel!" her mother called. "Don't you have to go to school today?"

"Okay, Mom, I'm coming." Rachel hugged her mom extra hard at the front door. "I'll see you after school. Have a *hoppy* day, Mom!"

Jerry was waiting for Rachel at the bus stop. "Guess what, Jerry? I get to keep Bunny! Do you want to help me build a cage for her?"

Jerry's mother interrupted his answer. "Jerry Welch!" his mother called from across the street. "Where's your hat?"

"My ears were sweating!" he called back. "I took it off."

Rachel wasn't wearing a hat, either. She'd washed her hair for the middle school tour, and her mom had blow-dried it. It was a little fluffy, and she didn't want to make it all flat and stringy again. Even Jerry had tidied up a bit. He wasn't wearing anything new, but his clothes were clean and ironed.

"Check this out," Jerry said. "My mom packed everything in newspapers when we moved." Jerry turned his pants pockets inside out. "Coupons! I have coupons for dog food, coffee, crackers, deodorant, everything you can think of." Jerry handed the pile of clippings to Rachel. "We'll be rich!"

Mrs. Jaeckel opened her apartment window and called down the street. "I'm expecting you two after school for brownies." Rachel saw Mrs. Angora waving down to them, too.

Rachel and Jerry waved back to them. "Okay, thanks!" they shouted.

While they were waiting for the bus, they talked about the trip to the middle school and what it would be like there next year.

"Hey, Jerry," said Rachel as the bus turned the corner. "Do you know what's going to be the best thing about middle school?"

"We'll have better lunches?" asked Jerry.

"No," Rachel groaned. "All you think about is food, Jerry Welch. The best thing is that the school's going to be so big, and there are going to be so many new kids there that we'll hardly ever see the Snob Squad. They probably won't be in any of our classes. We'll just forget all about them," said Rachel with a smile. "What a relief!"

They climbed on the bus and took their regular seats. As the bus pulled away, Jerry shouted, "Rachel, look over by that wall in the sunny spot. It's a yellow crocus! It's the first one of the year. That means spring is here!"

"You're right, Jerry," said Rachel looking at the first crocus of spring. "I wonder if it's warm enough to start my flower seeds growing?"

About the Author

SHERRY SHAHAN is married and has two daughters. She and her family live on a horse ranch called Hidden Oaks in California where they breed and raise racehorses. Sherry considers herself an "adventurer at heart." Every year, she and her husband take a special trip to a foreign land and explore the countryside on horseback. They have traveled across Argentina, Kenya, New Zealand, and Hawaii on horses.

Sherry has been a writer for 10 years. She gets her inspiration from everyday life with her own children. She also writes articles about her travels for magazines.

When Sherry is not busy writing or chauffering her children, she enjoys aerobics, jogging, and bicycling.